P9-ASF-835

BEWILDERED FOR THREE DAYS

As to Why Daniel Boone Never Wore His Coonskin Cap

BY ANDREW GLASS

Holiday House / New York

TO MARY CASH

Text and illustrations copyright © 2000 by Andrew Glass
All Rights Reserved
Printed in the United States of America
www.holidayhouse.com
First Edition

The art for this book was created with colored pencil and oil pastel.

The text typeface is Clearface Regular.

Library of Congress Cataloging-in-Publication Data

Glass, Andrew, 1949–
Bewildered for three days: as to why Daniel Boone never wore his coonskin cap / by Andrew Glass.—1st ed.
p. cm.
Summary: With the help of what he learned from a Delaware Indian boy and an accommodating mother raccoon, young Daniel Boone escapes danger when a bear steals his coonskin cap.
ISBN 0-8234-1446-9 (hardcover)
1. Boone, Daniel, 1734–1820—Childhood and youth—Juvenile fiction. [1. Boone, Daniel, 1734–1820—Childhood and youth—Fiction. 2. Frontier and pioneer life—Pennsylvania—Fiction. 3. Pennsylvania—Fiction.] I. Title.

PZ7.G48115 Be 2000
[E]—dc21   00-024344

One afternoon in 1818 an artist by the name of Chester Harding stopped by my cabin. He had it in mind to paint my portrait. I pulled on my worn buckskin britches, just like the ones I wore when first I ventured into the dark Allegheny Mountains to explore the howling wilderness of Kentucky.

"It is a puzzlement, sir. You dress in the buckskin of a backwoodsman, but where is your legendary coonskin cap?"

"It is true I'm often pictured so," I replied. "That is merely the invention of frontier storytellers. I've not worn any such head covering since I was a boy on the Pennsylvania frontier."

The poor man seemed sorely disappointed.

" 'Twas a solemn debt of gratitude. A promise, pure and simple," I replied. "Fact is, when I carved out the Wilderness Road to lead folks through the Cumberland Gap, I was wearing a wide-brimmed hat near as tall as this tale I'll tell ye to pass the time."

From the day I took my first step, I had the itching foot and was apt to wander off.

"Beware of braves in the forest!" Papa warned. "Should ye see strangers, Daniel, stand perfectly still until they pass."

When Papa called out "Cherokee!" my brothers and sisters and I all froze in our tracks like stones. It was a game.

Sometimes fierce bands of Cherokee crossed the distant blue mountains to raid scattered cabins at the edge of the wilderness. Here in this part of Pennsylvania, Quaker elders purchased their land fairly from the Delaware. But frontier peace was ever uneasy.

One day as my brothers and I were at work in our hardscrabble field, warriors burst through the trees, shrieking and waving hatchets. Folks screamed and snatched up little children. Women lifted their long skirts and sprinted for the log cabins. I tripped, but afore I could tumble, I was seized. Strong, copper-colored hands hurled me high in the air. I looked right into the fearsome dark eyes of a Delaware brave.

Nete-wata-wes spoke the King's English right smartly. "Word spread that you were under attack," he announced. "We ran to surprise your enemies."

Mama brushed my hair back from my forehead. "It was only a terrifying misunderstanding," she said.

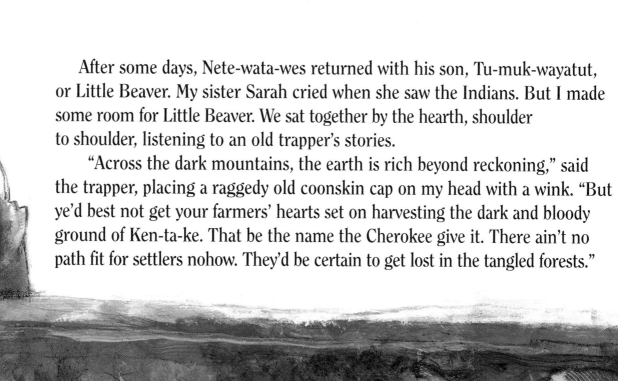

After some days, Nete-wata-wes returned with his son, Tu-muk-wayatut, or Little Beaver. My sister Sarah cried when she saw the Indians. But I made some room for Little Beaver. We sat together by the hearth, shoulder to shoulder, listening to an old trapper's stories.

"Across the dark mountains, the earth is rich beyond reckoning," said the trapper, placing a raggedy old coonskin cap on my head with a wink. "But ye'd best not get your farmers' hearts set on harvesting the dark and bloody ground of Ken-ta-ke. That be the name the Cherokee give it. There ain't no path fit for settlers nohow. They'd be certain to get lost in the tangled forests."

Nete-wata-wes spoke. "Our fathers told of the Warrior's Path. An entire people might cross together, but they would need a guide with the heart of a brave to lead them."

Little Beaver returned often. We wrestled and practiced tracking animals silently as shadows in the woods. Little Beaver taught me to listen well to the chatter, chirps, and croaks in the forest.

"Is this how I will find the heart of a brave?" I asked.

"No, it is the way to catch a squirrel," Little Beaver answered.

Little Beaver showed me how to wade streams, swing on wild grapevines, and walk on smooth rocks, leaving no tracks. I wanted to be just like him, and I took to dressing in skins and stuck feathers into the old trapper's coonskin cap. We played at painting ourselves for war and throwing the heavy hatchet.

Early one morning, as I bolted out the door, Papa grabbed me by the belt.
"See to thy chores and spend less time among Indians," he ordered.
"Yes sir," I answered, but my foot itched, and I scratched it with the other.
Little Beaver found me that day pounding corn into meal. He helped me tote water from the distant spring and collect wood chips for kindling.
Nete-wata-wes frowned at seeing his son sharing my chores. "It is time Little Beaver proved himself in the company of young Delaware braves," he told Papa.

But fathers cannot always keep a watchful eye to their sons. We often disappeared together deep into the woods. By then I could throw a hatchet as well as Little Beaver and out-wrestle him more often than not.

"Now do I have the heart of a brave?" I asked.

Little Beaver only shrugged.

"Thou art not an Indian boy, Daniel," Mama said. "It will soon be time for thee and Little Beaver to part ways."

"The Delaware are our betters in the ways of the wilderness," Papa said. "None can teach thee woodcraft as they can, but we measure off fields for farming and build fences. The Delaware live in the forest and love the savage wilderness as their mother. When we ask them to honor our fences, it is an unreasonable thing we ask. I fear there is no way to share a land so differently understood."

Soon Little Beaver was of an age to cut his long hair and take his place as a Delaware brave. So when Papa purchased grazing land far from our home, I was happy to go along with Mama to tend the scrawny cows. All the day long I wandered the forest in search of strays.

"Keep thy wits about thee, Daniel, and do not wander far," said Mama.

"Yes ma'am," said I. But saying so set my foot itching, and I scratched it.

I was never lonely. Each day took me farther and farther from home.

One afternoon I fell asleep in a mossy glade. I awoke to a malodorous sniffling and snorting.

A warm black nose glistened over me. A bear opened his hairy jaws wide and showed me his long teeth.

He snatched my cap, turned, and loped away. Now you'd likely think that I'd just have let that big old bear have the raggedy cap and count myself lucky that my head wasn't still in it. But that old cap meant something to me, so I trailed him.

He was easy enough to follow. Crows announced his passing from the
treetops, all the way to a high meadow where a commotion of wild turkeys
made the hill seem about to up and fly away. I never even saw the braves until
they saw me.

A way off the braves commenced to whoop and holler. I broke for the woods. But the braves chased me through the flapping turkeys, right to the edge of a sheer rock cliff. It fell some sixty feet to a rushing stream. Arrows whizzed by. When the braves got to throwing distance, a hatchet toppled past, end over end. What was I to do?

I leapt.

The braves howled as I crashed into the topmost branches of a sugar maple. They peered down from the cliff's edge. One waved the coonskin cap.

I slid down the trunk and swam downstream a goodly distance before wading ashore. Using every trick Little Beaver taught me, I zigzagged and circled to confound the trail.

By nightfall I thought I was beyond their reach, when I heard a commotion. The band of young braves was in good spirits, laughing heedlessly and hollering. A hiding place seemed the best course of action. I squirmed headfirst into a hollow log.

Two wide raccoon eyes shone in the dark and a passel of bright-eyed, blinking littl'uns. I had no hankering to drop in unexpected on a mama raccoon. She can be a scrappy critter if her little'uns are in danger. But there I was and there was no telling how long I'd be staying.

My heart pounded over the thuds and scrapes of wood being tossed onto a crackling campfire. I imagined the braves sitting right on top of me, roasting up a little supper, and making themselves comfortable under the twinkling stars.

The braves passed the best part of the night telling stories. It was damp and cold. My arms and legs were all cramped up and ached something awful. I was so dog tired I was near to drifting off anyway, when they commenced pounding the log like a war drum.

The braves, finally tired of their storytelling and after catching a few hours of sleep, continued their journey. But it seemed to me that the morning took an unnatural long time in coming.

I crawled backward into the cool damp of dawn. The critters also stirred.
"I don't know how to thank you for your hospitality, ma'am," I said to the
mama raccoon. "But this I promise, sure and solemn: I will never again wear
any of your kin on my head."

Before moving on, I carved a message in a tree near the hollow log that had sheltered us.

D. Boone made
a promise
1747

What with all the zigging and zagging and doubling back, I'd lost my bearings, and bedded down two more nights in the forest before finding my way home to Mama.

The painter daubed the last bits of color onto his canvas. He turned it around to show me the picture of myself holding a wide-brimmed hat.

"You mean to tell me that the great Daniel Boone was lost in the woods?" he asked.

"No sir," I replied. "I can't say that I was ever truly lost, only that I was bewildered for three days."

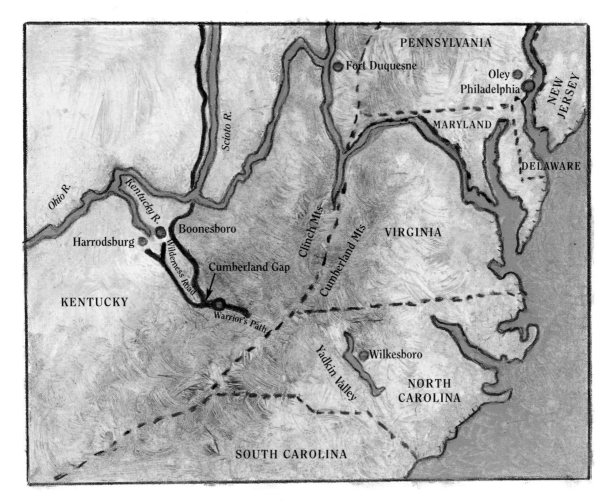

Author's Note

I began reading accounts of Daniel Boone's adventures, because unlike his contemporary Davy Crockett, who was a great self-promoter and storyteller, Daniel seemed a likable and modest sort of frontier folk hero. While looking for an incident that I might retell as a tall tale, I discovered that his legendary coonskin cap was invented by writers and artists. One account even said that he hated coonskin caps. Probably he preferred a wide-brimmed hat that would have kept the sun out of his eyes, but in the interest of yarn spinning I admit to inventing a more dramatic explanation.

Although a work of fiction, my tall tale is based in fact. It is true that Quaker settlers professed the equality of all people. As a young Quaker, Daniel would have been accustomed to living among American Indians. He might well have had a Delaware playmate. I chose names of the Delaware characters in my story from a list of names in Herbert C. Kraft's book *The Lenape or Delaware Indians*.

Somehow Daniel learned skills of wilderness survival so well that the *North American Review*, in 1846, referred to him as a "white Indian." He did in fact live with his mother during the sum-

mers from 1744 to about 1750, tending cows and wandering the woods alone, but both the bear incident and the death-defying leap are drawn from later tales about his adventures in Kentucky. The long night hiding in a hollow log is entirely my invention.

Daniel Boone was most likely born on November 2, 1734, although some accounts differ. He was the sixth of eleven children (seven sons and four daughters) born to Squire and Sarah Morgan Boone in Oley, Pennsylvania. Squire Boone was from a village near Exeter, England, and was a weaver by trade like his father and grandfather. He learned to be a blacksmith and a gunsmith, too.

Daniel was said to have been his mother's favorite. She would not listen to any criticism of his behavior. He had little formal schooling, but with improvised spelling he could write after a fashion. The messages Daniel carved in trees were generally misspelled. Woodcraft came naturally to him. By age ten he was one of the best woodsmen in the village. By fifteen he was considered the best. The British declared the eastern mountains off limits to settlers, but Daniel probably heard stories from trappers of Ken-ta-ke (called "the dark and bloody ground"), where the Cherokee and the Shawnee fought wars so violent that neither tribe dared actually live there.

About 1752, drawn by the prospect of abundant farmland, the Boone family began the difficult journey down the eastern side of the mountains through Virginia to settle at the very edge of the frontier, along the Yadkin River near Wilkesboro, North Carolina. In 1755, during the French and Indian War, Daniel joined the North Carolina militia as a supply wagon driver in General Braddock's disastrous attempt to drive the French out of Fort Duquesne (located in what is now Pittsburgh). He returned to North Carolina to marry Rebecca Bryan on August 14, 1756. She was sixteen. Daniel was almost twenty-two. Rebecca was an adventurous pioneer woman, but when her young husband told her they were moving to Florida, near Pensacola, she said no, refusing to live among alligators and snakes.

Over the next several years, Daniel began exploring the Cumberland Mountains. Some accounts have him in 1760 all the way to what would become Tennessee. But for sure in 1769, Boone accompanied his friend John Finley to explore Kentucky.

By 1773, the Boones set off along with about a dozen other families to attempt to settle Kentucky. By then the Boones had been married for seventeen years and had nine children: James and Israel (who were both killed in battles with the Shawnee), Jesse, Daniel, Nathan, Susan, Jemima, Lavina, and Rebecca. The group turned back after James was killed. In 1775, Daniel crossed the Clinch Mountains with thirty well-armed men. They passed through the Cumberland Gap and enlarged the Warrior's Path, building a new Wilderness Road through the open plains of Kentucky. Where Otter Creek flows into the Kentucky River, they built log cabins and a stockade and called their settlement Boonesboro. Daniel returned for his family later that year. The Boones were the first pioneer family to settle in Kentucky. However, James Harrod built the first log cabin settlement, called Harrodsburg, in the summer of 1774. Kentucky was made a county of Virginia in 1776 as the American Revolution began.

Not everyone was happy to see the western frontier opened to settlers. The Shawnee, under Chief Blackfish, allied themselves with the British, hoping to undercut western settlement. When a group of girls, including Daniel's daughter Jemima, were kidnapped, the story of their rescue made the forty-year-old Daniel Boone a frontier hero in the East. Daniel was made a captain of the new militia. In 1718, when he was taken prisoner, the Shawnee showed their respect by making him a member of their tribe, calling him Big Turtle. He escaped just in time to save Boonesboro from attack.

His family, thinking him dead, returned to North Carolina, but they returned with him to establish Boone's Station in 1779. Meanwhile Daniel's legend spread after the publication in 1784 of *The Discovery, Settlement and Present State of Kentucky* by John Filson, which told of his adventures. Daniel served in the Virginia Legislature, but he was not a successful government official. During the War of 1812 he volunteered and was surprised to be told he was too old. He was only seventy-eight.

He went on roaming the farthest wilderness all the way to Yellowstone, often in the company of an unnamed Indian companion. *The Adventures of Daniel Boone* by his nephew Daniel Bryan was published in 1813, the same year that Boone's wife died. He buried Rebecca on a mound in St. Charles County overlooking the Missouri River.

Daniel was eighty years old in 1814 when the U.S. Congress granted him a thousand acres of the nine thousand he once laid claim to in upper Louisiana. He sold them to pay his debts and then went hunting.

After Rebecca's death, Daniel lived in the homes of his children, carving powder horns, repairing rifles, and telling stories to his grandchildren. One day an artist named Chester Harding, with a commission to paint Daniel Boone's portrait, appeared at the house of his son Nathan Boone in St. Charles, Missouri. The artist later recounted that he found the old man living alone in a cabin. Upon learning that the explorer never carried a compass, he asked Daniel if he'd ever been lost. The woodsman replied, "No, I was never lost, but I was bewildered for three days." On September 26, 1820, Daniel Boone died, and he was buried next to Rebecca Boone. He was eighty-six years old. They were reburied together in Frankfort, Kentucky, in 1845, overlooking the Kentucky River.

Selected Bibliography

Alexander, Kent. *American Folklore and Legend*. Pleasantville, New York: Readers Digest Association, Inc., 1978.

———. *Heroes of the Wild West*. New York: Mallard Press, 1992.

Battle, Kemp P., compiler. *Great American Folklore*. New York: Barnes & Noble, 1986.

Beiting, Fr. Ralph W. *Soldier of the Revolution: A New View of Daniel Boone*. Lancaster, Kentucky: Christian Appalachian Project, 1977.

Blakeless, John. *Daniel Boone: Master of the Wilderness*. New York: William Morrow & Company, 1939.

Boone, Daniel and Francis L. Hawks. *Daniel Boone: His Own Story and the Adventures of Daniel Boone: The Kentucky Rifleman*. Bedford, Massachusetts: Applewood Books, 1996.

Brown, John Mason. *Daniel Boone: The Opening of the Wilderness*. New York: Random House, 1952.

Cattermole, A. B., and E. G. *Famous Frontiersmen Pioneers and Scouts: The Vanguards of American Civilization*. Chicago, Illinois: Donohue, Henneberry & Company, circa 1880.

Cunningham, Daniel. *The Story of Daniel Boone*. New York: Doubleday and Company, Inc., 1952. Abridged from *The Real Book About Daniel Boone*. New York: Franklin Watts Inc., 1952.

Kraft, Herbert C. *The Lenape or Delaware Indians*. South Orange, New Jersey: Seton Hall University Museum, 1991.

White, Stewart Edward. *Daniel Boone: Wilderness Scout*. Garden City, New York: Doubleday, Page and Company, 1922.